For Laura
May You Always
Be Protected by the
Sewanee Angels
Beth Charlton ♥

The owner of this book

_____

is protected by the
Sewanee Angels

ISBN 978-1493731879

Available from Amazon.com and other book stores.

For permission to reproduce any part of this book:

infosewaneeangels@gmail.com

1114 Red Oak Drive, Monteagle TN 37356

Printed in the USA

November 11, 2013

The Adventures of the Sewanee Angels

By Beth Charlton
&
Margaret H. Matens

Illustrated by
Margaret H. Matens

THE DOMAIN OF
THE UNIVERSITY
OF THE SOUTH

A Tennessee town was picked long ago
For the site of a college up on a plateau.
The first students came on the Mountain Goat Train,
Arriving in Sewanee's vast wooded Domain.
When buildings of log and stone were erected,
The angels agreed that they should be protected.
Otey Hall, Quintard, and old Rebel's Rest …
The campus was founded and by Bishops blessed.
According to legend, those inside the gates
Are guarded each night, so no trouble awaits.

The littlest angels sleep soundly
all day,
At nighttime they wake up and
come out to play!

They watch every child,
   every deer, every dog ...
In all four seasons, in moonlight and fog.
All over Sewanee they romp and have fun,
They don't stop their mischief
   'til they see the sun.

They fly over Sewanee, where stores line the street
Post office, gas station, places to eat.
There's shopping at Taylor's and at Lemon Fair,
Friends at Shenanigans and The Blue Chair.

And named in their honor,
the new Angel Park!
A great place to gather
for fun in the dark.

The children of Sewanee are proud of their school
Where kindness and sharing are always the rule.
The angels come visit to zip down the slide
And borrow the books they discover inside.
They love to read stories for hours each night
With lanterns of fireflies and stars for their light.

There's Otey Parish, stone church on a hill,
A refuge in summers and in winters chill.
Historical site for a century and more ...
The Episcopal Church with a wide
open door.

They perch on the spires of
    McClurg and on Guerry,
Looking down on dark halls,
    on the dorms and library.
They love to see All Saints' —
    its stained glass and arches,
In May it's the place where each
    graduate marches.
Weddings are blessed —
    just hear the bells ringing,
Then Lessons and Carols with
    its joyful singing.

Into the bookstore, to see
   what is new,
Gear for each sports team,
   field hockey to crew.
There's purple galore,
   an alumni delight;
"It's not a river" and
   "Yea Sewanee's Right!"

Just like the angels, the night-loving critters
Come out at dark, and some bring their litters.
Raccoon and possum, flying squirrel, fox,
Wake up every night by their nocturnal clocks.
An angel says, "Listen... a coyote's howl!"
Then off they go flying, now chasing an owl.

On summer nights they love Abbo's Alley,
A favorite spot to just dilly-dally.
At night it is magic with fireflies agleam,
With bridges that criss-cross the silvery
    stream.
The maple and oak trees stretch high up
    like towers,
Below nestle ferns and a flourish of flowers.

First called St. Lukes'— now the School
    of Theology,
Where all seminarians sing the Doxology.
They live in the Woodlands, all tucked
    tight together
And stand by each other in all kinds of
    weather.

The Cross is a beacon
  set on the bluff's rim,
The angels start singing
  an old battle hymn,
Showing respect for
  the soldiers who died,
Below lies the valley,
  its fields stretching wide.

McGee Field in fall means football so fine …
A legend begun in 1899.
A group of top colleges all Sewanee bested,
And then… "On the seventh day"… well, they just rested!

On coldest nights in the dead of the winter
The angels play games in the warm Fowler Center.
Up on the diving board one angel swoops,
There's tennis and track and
    a group playing hoops.

The golf course and Green's View
    are wrapped in a cloud,
The angels can't see so they must
    shout aloud.
"Don't get lost!" "Over Here!"
    It is one misty maze...
They play hide and seek in
    the fog and the haze.

Over Lake Cheston's wide surface they skim,
A summertime favorite to picnic and swim.
The turtles and frogs are great fun to chase …
Then off to the stable. Let's make it a race!

The Equestrian Center is
barnloads of fun,
With horses of dapple and
chestnut and dun.

As one leads the way, through forests
they follow,
On Perimeter Trail and down Shakerag Hollow.
Buggy Top, Lost Cove and steep
Bridal Veil …
They're liking night hiking beneath the
moon pale.

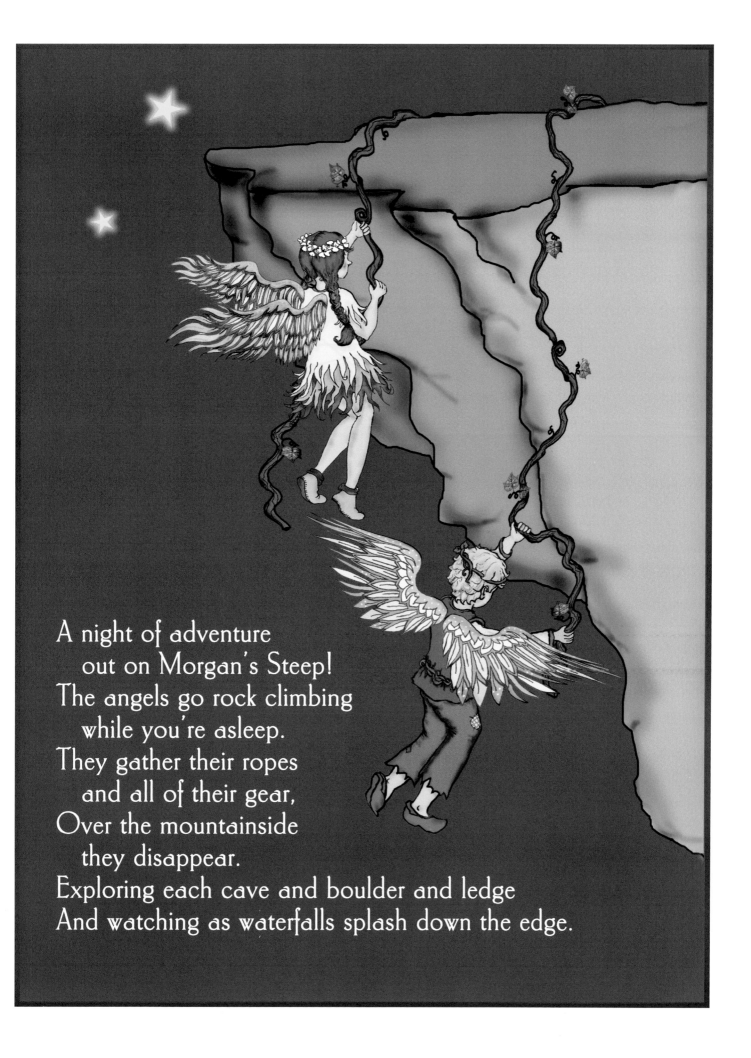

A night of adventure
   out on Morgan's Steep!
The angels go rock climbing
   while you're asleep.
They gather their ropes
   and all of their gear,
Over the mountainside
   they disappear.
Exploring each cave and boulder and ledge
And watching as waterfalls splash down the edge.

It's been a long night, and the little ones yawn,
The morning star rises, not long until dawn!
From above angels watch over all that surrounds …
Monteagle to Beersheba, neighboring towns.
St. Andrew's-Sewanee, St. Mary's, DuBose,
Assembly and Clifftops — all's in repose.
The bluffs, parks and waterfalls of the Plateau …
All of God's beauty is spread out below.

They've played and explored, but
their job's not neglected,
These angels make sure that you're
always protected!

When you drive out the gates,
    grab an angel, reach high.
One follows with you,
    the rest wave goodbye.

Though you travel far from the
Sewanee you love,
Be at peace, guardian angels will
watch from above.

THE END